Noddy Goes Shopping

HarperCollins *Children's Books*

It was a peaceful morning in Toy Town…

PARP! PARP! The startled folk of Toy Town looked up as Noddy's car hurtled through the streets.

"We made it!" gasped Mrs Skittle as the car screeched to a halt at the station.

"Now, Noddy," she said. "How much do I owe you?"

Noddy wasn't sure.

"Um, did I say two children count as one grown up, or…"

"Noddy!" cried Mrs Skittle. "I don't have time for this. Here! Keep the change." And she dropped a heap of coins into his hand.

"Oh!" cried Noddy. "What a lot of money!"

Noddy jumped into his car and zoomed across
town to Big-Ears' house.

"Hello, Big-Ears!" cried Noddy, running
up the stairs. "I've just earned loads of money.
We could go out and spend it on... oh!"

He stopped in surprise.

Big-Ears was still in bed!

"Big-Ears! It's the middle of the morning and you're still asleep!" said Noddy.

"I wish I *was* asleep," Big-Ears yawned, loudly. "That's the problem. I just can't seem to get to sleep at all."

"Then why don't you go to bed early?" suggested Noddy.

"I can't get to sleep!" said Big-Ears, crossly. "If I weren't so tired, I'd go into town to buy the things I need to make a sleeping charm."

"*I'll* go for you!" cried Noddy.

"That's very kind," said Big-Ears. "Now, listen: I'll need a small cloth bag to hold everything."

"Small cloth bag," repeated Noddy. "Got it."

"A bunch of night-blooming flowers to make me feel sleepy."

"OK," said Noddy. "What else?"

Big-Ears thought hard. "A small black stone,
to make my eyes feel heavy."

"Right," said Noddy. "Small black stone."

"And a few little white balls of cotton wool
to use as ear plugs. Oh, yes, and a torch,
to remind me of the calming moonlight."

"You must remember all the things," said Big-Ears.
"If you forget just one of them, the charm
won't work."

"Don't worry, Big-Ears!" said Noddy.

Big-Ears yawned. "And I also need a
toy saw," he said. "It'll get me snoring."

"Six things," said Noddy, as he headed for the door. "I'll remember all of them!"

Big-Ears checked the time. "Noddy should be back in about half an hour."

And he settled back to wait.

One hour and forty-five minutes later,
Noddy had still not come back.

"Where on earth *is* Noddy?" yawned
Big-Ears. "He should be back by now."

The clock ticked away.

But still Noddy did not come back.
Big-Ears grew more and more worried.

Just then, he heard the front door open,
and the sound of eager footsteps coming
up the stairs.

"I'm back!" cried Noddy, bursting into the room.
"What took you so long?" asked Big-Ears.
"Sorry," said Noddy, dumping a large box on
the floor. "It just took a while to get all six things."

"Here's the cloth bag," said Noddy,
pulling a large sack out of the box.
Big-Ears peered into it.
"I can't see any little bag.
Are you sure it's in here?"

"It's not *in* the sack," laughed Noddy. "It *is* the sack!"

"Noddy," groaned Big-Ears, "I said a *small* bag."

"Oops!" said Noddy. "Does it matter? Surely, the bigger the better?"

Big-Ears sighed.

"What about the ear plugs?" asked Big-Ears.

Noddy handed Big-Ears some hard white balls.

"Oh, no! Not golf balls!" wailed Big-Ears.

"I said *cotton wool* balls."

Noddy shrugged. "All I could remember
was white balls. Sorry!"

Big-Ears shook his head. "Well, Noddy… did you remember the small black stone?"

Noddy pulled a big, grey rock out of the box.

"Honestly, Noddy," frowned Big-Ears.

"I said a small black stone. This is big and grey!"

"Oh, dear. I forgot about the size," said Noddy, "but I didn't forget the colour!"

He pulled out a black pencil and started scribbling on the rock.

"Have you remembered *anything* properly?" moaned Big-Ears.

Noddy put his hand back into the box.

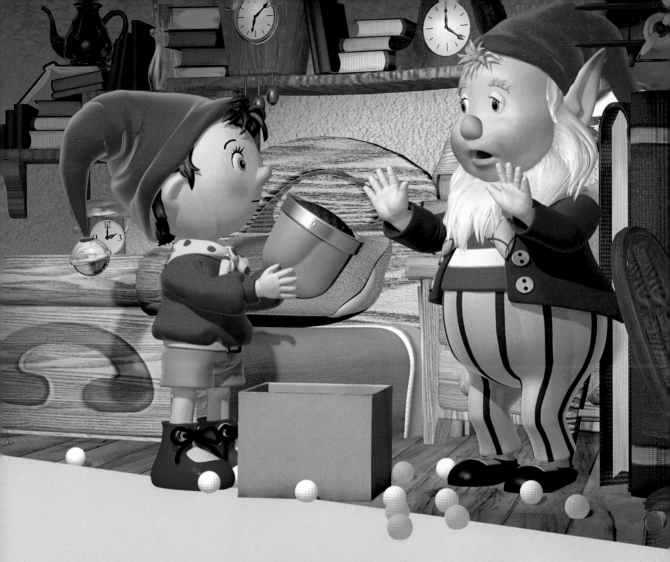

"What is that for?" asked Big-Ears, crossly.

"A car headlight for your moonlight, silly!"
said Noddy. "Now *you* don't remember!"

"No, no, no, no, *no!*" cried Big-Ears. "I said
a *torch*, not a *headlight*."

"Won't a headlight do?" asked Noddy.

"Well, at least I remembered the tool to make you snore!" said Noddy.

Big-Ears couldn't believe Noddy had been so silly. "I said *saw*, Noddy. Not *spanner*."

"Oh dear! What a bad memory I have," said Noddy. "But look, you could try this…" And he put the spanner on his nose.

Big-Ears pulled the spanner off Noddy's nose.

"I expect you've muddled up the flowers as well," sighed Big-Ears.

Noddy put his hand into the box and pulled out a bunch of dead weeds.

"Wrong!" groaned Big-Ears. "Just like everything else!"

"Noddy," Big-Ears said sadly, "you didn't remember one single thing."

Noddy hung his head.

"I'm really sorry, Big-Ears," he said. "I just don't have a very good memory."

Big-Ears smiled. "No, you don't. But you do have a good forgetery!"

Noddy sighed in relief. "Thank goodness you're not really cross, Big-Ears. I tried my best, truly I did."

"I know," said Big-Ears. "But if you need to remember something, write it down."

"What a good idea!" whooped Noddy, happily.

Big-Ears quickly wrote out a shopping list.

"Thanks," said Noddy. "Now I'll remember everything!" And he picked up the box and rushed downstairs.

Seconds later, he was back.

"Err… I forgot the list, Big-Ears," he said, as he grabbed it.

Big-Ears grinned as he shuffled back to bed.

"That boy… Oops!" Big-Ears' foot slipped on a golf ball.

BOING! He hit the bed and then bounced up to the ceiling. THWACK! Down he came with a mighty THUD! Big-Ears was out cold!

A little while later, Noddy came back.
   "I managed to get everything on the list!"
he called. "Now you can get some sleep, Big-Ears.
   … oh!"
He stopped, staring in astonishment.

"Zzzz-zzzz-zzzz." Big-Ears was fast asleep,
snoring loudly. He looked very comfortable.
Noddy crept over to the bed.
"Maybe you didn't need the sleeping
charm after all," he whispered.

"Good night!" said Noddy, and he pulled
the bedcovers gently over Big-Ears
and tiptoed out.

"Zzzzzzzzzzzzz…"

First published in Great Britain by HarperCollins Publishers Ltd in 2003
This edition published by HarperCollins Children's Books
HarperCollins Children's Books is a division of HarperCollins Publishers Ltd.

ISBN-10: 0-00-778465-1
ISBN-13: 978-0-00-778465-3

Visit our website at: www.harpercollinschildrensbooks.co.uk

Printed and bound by Printing Express Ltd, Hong Kong